VAN GOOL'S

Just So Stories

THE ELEPHANT'S CHILD
THE BUTTERFLY THAT STAMPED
HOW THE LEOPARD GOT HIS SPOTS

SMITHMARK

THE ELEPHANT'S CHILD

Many, many years ago, O Best Beloved, the elephant had no trunk. He had only a short little nose, hardly bigger than a boot. He could wriggle it a little, but could not pick anything up with it. At this time, there lived in Africa an Elephant's Child, who was full of insatiable curiosity. He was always asking questions. He asked questions of everyone – his parents, the Ostrich, the Hippopotamus, the Giraffe and the Baboon. Soon everyone was tired of his questions, and they spanked him with their paws, their hooves and their feet.

One fine morning, the Elephant's Child asked a question he'd never asked before. He asked, "What does the Crocodile eat for his dinner?" And all the animals turned on him in horror. "Hush!" they cried, and spanked him for a long time for asking such a question.

Later the Elephant's Child met Kolokolo Bird. "Everyone spanks me for being so curious," he told Kolokolo. "But all the same, I would like to know what the Crocodile eats for his dinner!"

Then Kolokolo said to him, "Go to the great, green Limpopo River, which is as deep as the sea, and bordered with fever trees. There you will find an answer."

The next day the Elephant's Child took a hundred pounds of bananas, a hundred pounds of sugar cane and seventeen melons, and announced to his family, "I am going to the great, green Limpopo River which is as deep as the sea, and bordered with fever trees. There I will find out what the Crocodile eats for his dinner." The animals gathered around him and spanked him for good luck.

He set off on his way, eating melons,
and leaving the rinds where they fell,
for he could not pick them up.

After a long walk, he arrived at the great, green Limpopo River, which was as deep as the sea, and bordered with fever trees, exactly as Kolokolo had said. Here he met a Bi-Colored-Python-Rock-Snake curled around a rock, and asked, "Excuse me, do you know what the Crocodile eats for his dinner?" Immediately the Bi-Colored-Python-Rock-Snake uncoiled himself and began to spank the Elephant's Child with his long tail, for asking such a question.

When the snake had finished, the Elephant's Child said good-bye very politely, and walked along the banks of the Limpopo to try and find the Crocodile. He had never seen a Crocodile before, so did not know what one was like, but he was very curious.

Suddenly the Elephant's Child saw what he thought was a log floating on the river. But this was really the Crocodile, who lazily opened one eye, and flexed his long tail.

Believing he was going to be spanked again, the Elephant's Child backed away, then asked, "Excuse me, could you tell me where I might find the Crocodile?" "Why, child, I am the Crocodile," replied the Crocodile. And he wept a few crocodile tears to show that it was true.

The Elephant's Child was overjoyed, and asked, "Please tell me, what do you eat for your dinner?"

"Come closer, my child," said the Crocodile softly. "I want to whisper in your ear."

So the Elephant's Child lowered his head until it was next to the Crocodile's sharp teeth. Suddenly the Crocodile opened his mouth and seized the Elephant's Child's little nose, which was no bigger than a boot.

"I believe," hissed the Crocodile through his teeth, "that today, I will begin my dinner with an Elephant's Child!"

At these words, the Elephant's Child was terrified. "Led go of be," he honked through his nose. "You're hurting be!"

But the Crocodile slid back into the water, and began to pull and pull, splashing in the river with his long tail. And the Elephant's Child pulled and pulled, until slowly his nose began to stretch. Then he felt his legs slipping.

The Bi-Colored-Python-Rock-Snake slithered quickly to the riverbank, and wrapping his tail around the back legs of the Elephant's Child, he began to pull. The Elephant's Child pulled and pulled, and his nose stretched even further. And still the Crocodile pulled. But between them, the Elephant's Child and the python pulled the hardest, and the Crocodile finally let go. He fell back into the water with a loud splash that could be heard all along the Limpopo.

The Elephant's Child thanked the python very much, then he wrapped his poor nose in cool banana leaves, and bathed it in the river. "I'm waiting for it to shrink," he explained.

"You'll be there forever!" said the python, adding, "Some people don't know their own luck."

The Elephant's Child stayed there for three days, but his nose didn't shrink.

Towards the end of the third day, a fly landed on his shoulder. Without even thinking about it, the Elephant's Child swatted the fly with his new trunk.

"Advantage number one," remarked the Bi-Colored-Python-Rock-Snake. "Now, why don't you try and eat something?"

Without stopping to think, the Elephant's Child stretched out his trunk, grabbed a bunch of tasty leaves, and put them into his mouth.

"Advantage number two," said the Bi-Colored-Python-Rock-Snake. "By the way, don't you think the sun's a little warm?"

The Elephant's Child went to the river and sucked in a trunkful of mud. Then he splashed the cool mud all over his head and back.

"Advantage number three," said the clever Bi-Colored-Python-Rock-Snake.

"You couldn't have done those things with a teeny nose," said the wise Bi-Colored-Python-Rock-Snake. "And now, wouldn't you like to spank someone?"

"I should like to very much!" said the Elephant's Child.

"Well, you should find your new trunk very handy."

The Elephant's Child thanked the Bi-Colored-Python-Rock-Snake once more, and returned to his home across Africa. As he travelled he practised all the things he could do with his new trunk.

When he finally reached his home, the Elephant's Child walked up to his family. He curled up his trunk so they could not see it, and said, "Good evening." They were very happy to see him, and wanted to spank him at once for his insatiable curiosity.

But the Elephant's Child uncurled his trunk, and before they knew what was happening, he spanked them all.

"Where did you learn that trick?" they asked. "And what has happened to your nose?"

"I asked the Crocodile what he ate for dinner, and he made this nose for me," said the Elephant's Child. "It's very useful."

So one by one, the elephants went to the great, green Limpopo River, which is as deep as the sea and bordered with fever trees. There they asked the Crocodile to give each of them a new nose too.

And when they came home, no one spanked anyone any more. Since then, O Best Beloved, all elephants have had trunks, just like that of the curious Elephant's Child.

THE BUTTERFLY THAT STAMPED

Listen, O Best Beloved, to a story of Suleiman-bin-Daoud, who was a good and wise king. He also had magic powers: when he twisted the ring on his finger, genies would come out of the ground, ready to obey his every command. He lived in a huge golden palace, in the middle of a beautiful garden, with his 999 wives. This does not include Balkis, his favorite queen, who was nearly as wise as he. The 999 wives were always quarrelling with the king. Balkis was the only one who didn't argue with him. She loved him too much.

One day, after the 999 wives had been quarrelling with him ceaselessly for three weeks, Suleiman went out into the gardens for some peace and quiet. There he found Balkis, who begged him to twist his ring, so that the genies would appear. This would show his scolding wives what a great and terrible king he was.

But Suleiman said, "I cannot use my powers just to show off. That would be wrong."

And Suleiman sat down to rest at the foot of a camphor tree. Balkis moved away a little, so as not to disturb him. Soon, two butterflies arrived, and began to argue. "How dare you speak to me like that!" said one to the other. "If you do not hold your tongue, I will stamp my foot, and the king's golden palace will disappear in a crash of thunder!"

Hearing this boast, Suleiman let out a great shout of laughter. He called to the butterfly and asked, "Why did you tell your wife such an enormous lie?"

"She argues with me all the time," replied the butterfly, "and I hoped that it would keep her quiet."

Suleiman wished him good luck, and the butterfly flew back to his wife. "What did the king say to you?" asked the butterfly's wife.

The butterfly replied importantly, "The king loves his palace and his gardens very much, and begged me not to stamp my foot. Of course I promised I wouldn't."

"My goodness," said his wife, very impressed.

Balkis had heard everything, and had an idea of how to help her husband. She called to the female butterfly. "Do you believe your husband?" asked Balkis.

"Of course not," replied the butterfly. "But men are always boasting."

"You are quite right," said Balkis. "The next time your husband boasts about his powers, tell him to stamp. Then he will feel ashamed of himself."

41

Five minutes later, the butterflies were arguing worse than ever. "If I hadn't made a promise to the king you'd be sorry!" threatened the butterfly.

"I don't believe a word!" cried his wife. "Show me what you can do. Go on, stamp your foot!"

Suleiman had forgotten all about his 999 wives. "What am I to do?" the butterfly asked the king. "My wife will never listen to me again."

"Go ahead, little one," replied the king, "stamp your foot. My palace will disappear. Stamp your foot again, and it will return." So the Butterfly stamped his foot. At the same time, the king twisted his ring. At once genies appeared out of the ground.

At the king's command, the genies lifted the palace and the gardens a thousand miles into the air, with a great crash of thunder. The king's 999 wives shrieked and shouted from inside the palace.

Terrified, the butterfly's wife turned to her husband and begged him to do something, and promised that she would never argue with him again.

While Suleiman roared with laughter, the butterfly stamped his foot a second time, and the palace and the gardens reappeared.

No sooner had the palace returned, than the king's 999 wives came running out, demanding to know what had happened. "What was that terrible noise?" they cried. "Why did everything go dark?"

Balkis stepped out from her hiding place and stood before them. "It was just a little lesson that the king has given to the wife of his friend the butterfly, because she wouldn't stop quarrelling with him."

The 999 wives were very worried. If the king did this for a simple butterfly, what was he going to do to them? And they returned, in silence, to the palace.

Balkis told the king how she had made him use his magic powers. "Now you will have a peaceful life," she said. "Your 999 wives have learned their lesson."

Suleiman was astonished. Balkis had used his game with the two little butterflies to save him from his wives' endless arguments. "Oh, my favorite wife," he said to Balkis, "how did you become so wise?"

And Balkis looked into Suleiman's eyes and said, "It is because I love you, my husband!"

HOW THE LEOPARD GOT HIS SPOTS

At the beginning of time, O Best Beloved, the Giraffe, the Zebra, the Eland and the Kudu were all a sandy, yellowy-gray color, from their heads to their toes. But the Leopard was the sandiest and yellowest of them all. He could not be seen against the sand, the sun-baked rocks or the scrubby yellow bushes of the African plain. He could hide among the rocks and the bushes, and leap out on the other animals, who always got a terrible shock, because they had not seen him at all.

Also at this time there lived an Ethiopian, who was also sandy yellow, and he hunted with the Leopard. The other animals never knew when the Leopard or the Ethiopian were going to jump out on them. Finally, the animals became so tired of being hunted all the time that they went to find another place to live, where they might be left in peace. The Leopard and the Ethiopian found themselves running all around the plain, wondering where all their breakfasts and dinners had gone. They began to get very hungry indeed.

Meanwhile, the other animals had come to a huge forest. The sun shone through the trees and cast stripy, speckly shadows on the ground. After hiding themselves in the shadows for a while, the animals changed. The Giraffe grew great splotches, the Zebra grew dark stripes and the Eland and the Kudu grew darker, with little wavy lines on their backs. When they stood among the trees, you could not see them at all.

The Ethiopian and the Leopard were getting hungrier and hungrier, and one day they met Baviaan, the oldest, wisest Baboon in Africa. He told them that the animals were hiding in the forest.

The Leopard and the Ethiopian travelled to the big forest, where the animals were hiding. The shadowy forest was mainly dark, yet full of little pieces of light. The Leopard and the Ethiopian were very confused, because although they could smell the Giraffe, the Zebra, the Eland and the Kudu, they could not see them at all.

Among the dark shadows in the forest, the sandy-yellow Leopard, and the sandy-yellow Ethiopian were easy to see, and the animals had no trouble hiding from them. So they waited until the sun went down, and began hunting again. But although they could smell the animals, they still could not see them. Finally the Ethiopian and the Leopard captured an animal each, and waited until morning to see what they'd caught.

The Leopard and the Ethiopian were so surprised to
see how the Giraffe and the Zebra had changed, that
they let them go. The Giraffe and the Zebra ran into
the shadowy forest, and the shocked Ethiopian and
Leopard watched as their breakfast disappeared. The
Ethiopian was very impressed, and decided that he
would change his skin too.

He decided upon a deep browny-black color so that he could hide in the shadows and behind the trees. The Ethiopian advised the Leopard to change his skin too. "Why not spots?" he suggested. "They work very well for the Giraffe." But the Leopard did not want to look like any of the other animals.

The Ethiopian still had some color left from changing his own skin, and with his fingertips he made spots for the Leopard, five little spots at a time. Soon the Leopard was covered in dark spots, which made him very difficult to see in the mottled light of the forest.

"Now you are a beauty!" said the Ethiopian, standing back and admiring the Leopard's sleek skin. "Now come along and let us find our breakfast!"

So they went together into the forest, O Best Beloved, and hunted and played together forever after.